Published by Top That! Publishing plc
Tide Mill Way, Woodbridge, Suffolk, IP12 1AP, UK
www.topthatpublishing.com
Text copyright © Peter Francis-Browne 2010
Illustrated by Rita Gianetti
All rights reserved
0 2 4 6 8 9 7 5 3 1
Printed and bound in China

Creative Director – Simon Couchman
Editorial Director – Daniel Graham

Illustrated by Rita Gianetti
Written by Peter Francis-Browne

ISBN 978-1-84956-100-6

A catalogue record for this book is available from the British Library
Printed and bound in China

TOUCAN
TOUCAN'T

Text copyright © Peter Francis-Browne

Illustrated by Rita Gianetti

Toucan tango.

Toucan't share a potty.

Toucan see-saw.

Toucan't be king of the castle.

Toucan share a joke.

Toucan't keep a secret.

Toucan tickle.

Toucan't be first in line.

Toucan bang on a drum.

Toucan't ever be alone.

Toucan laze
under the Sun.

Toucan't cycle to the Moon.

Toucan make a butterfly
seem very small.

Toucan't form a football team.

Toucan float on giant lily pads.

Toucan't frighten a great, big tiger.

Toucan make feathers fly.

Toucan't share the same dream.

Toucan crunch a bunch
of the hardest nuts.

Toucan't make an ice cream sundae.

Toucan live in
the tallest trees.

Toucan't swim with crocodiles.

But, whatever happens,
toucan be friends forever.